*Plantation Child
and Other Stories*

Plantation Child and Other Stories

Eve Begley Kiehm

Illustrated by Christine Joy Pratt

A Kolowalu Book
University of Hawai'i Press • Honolulu

©1995 University of Hawai'i Press
All rights reserved
Printed in Singapore

00 99 98 97 96 95   5 4 3 2 1

Library of Congress Cataloging-in-Publication Data
Kiehm, Eve Begley, 1933–
    Plantation child and other stories / Eve Begley Kiehm.
    p.   cm.
"A Kolowalu book."
    Contents: Plantation child — The gulch is calling — Guava sticks
— Joe and the white dog — The little people — The pineapple cannery
— Abuji.
    ISBN 0-8248-1596-3
    1. Children's stories, American. [1. Korean Americans — Fiction.
2. Hawaii — Fiction. 3. Short stories.] I. Title.
PZ7.K539PL   1995   94-33410
[Fic] — dc20   CIP
                                                        AC

Designed by Paula Newcomb

For my four children
And for Dennis and the Kiehm family,
who have enriched my life

CONTENTS

*Plantation Child
and Other Stories*

Plantation Child

It was cooler in the canefield. Marita squeezed her small body through the stalks to find a safe place to hide. She had run all the way from the Korean camp with the sound of her father's angry voice in her ears.

"You spend eight dollars for shoes—eight dollars when I tell you I get only ten?"

He had reached out to slap her and she ran, knowing he was right, knowing she should not have bought such expensive shoes. But they were the first shoes she had ever had in her life, and surely for eighth-grade graduation she must look nice?

She scrunched down under the sheltering sugarcane and placed the shoes on her lap. They were nothing special—just ordinary brown leather shoes with a strap across the foot. But they had felt good enough to walk in. After fourteen years of going barefoot, most shoes were uncomfortable.

Mrs. Chun at the company store had said, "Get the shoes big enough. Tight shoes no good."

Marita had small feet—small like the rest of her. At fourteen she was the oldest in the family of five children but not the biggest.

She pulled the right shoe on her dusty foot and held it out to examine critically. It looked okay. Nice, even. Well, at least she wouldn't graduate barefoot. And after graduation she would get a job somewhere—maybe in Honolulu—and make money to buy her own shoes.

It was hard to believe graduation was so close. It seemed she had gone to school for a lifetime. Every day she left the camp at six in the morning, went to Korean school until seven thirty, then walked three miles to town with the others to elementary school. She stayed there until two, then walked back home. More Korean school at the camp. Then fix dinner at home and sometimes back to Korean school in the evening to memorize characters. And it was so hard to remember all these characters . . . How could Mama have learned so many? Sometimes she allowed herself to remember her mother, bringing out old memories from behind a shutter in her head and looking at each one before pushing it back behind the shutter: Mama with the sweet face looking down at her on the boat from Korea; Mama singing a song; Mama clutching her hand tightly as they went to meet the man who was to be her new father. He had taken them back to a small frame house on the edge of the canefields, in a camp where the Korean field-workers lived. The houses were roughly made, raised up on low platforms with a few steps up to the front doors. She remembered Mama making curtains from old rice sacks to cover the windows. And always she remembered herself carrying babies up and down the steps even when they were too heavy for her small arms to support them. All the brothers and sisters . . . one a year from the time she, Marita, was three years old. Mama seemed to get smaller and frailer while Marita grew bigger and stronger.

One memory thrust itself at her again and again, and she felt the tears forming as always: Mama taking her by the hand when she was about seven years old and opening the big trunk from Korea.

"See, daughter, I save clothes to wear when we go back to Korea, you and me. We take your brothers and sisters to see my family."

And she showed her the dark Korean skirt (*chi'ima*, Mama said) and white blouse (*chokori*) with the full sleeves, carefully folded and saved for years. But Mama never went back to Korea because she died one month after the last baby. "Afterbirth fever," the midwife said.

Nothing was the same after Mama died. Marita was the new mother, who fixed meals and washed clothes for the children and Papa. Some mother, she thought. Only eight years old.

"How you cook rice?" she asked her father that first day when he had told her to fix dinner. She had seen her mother wash the raw rice and put it in a pot on the fire in the compound. It had looked easy. Turned out to be not so easy. She never got the heat right and never could fix the wood right so the temperature under the pot was low and steady. The first night her father slapped her because the rice was not ready and he was hungry.

"I work half the night and half the day and need food," he grumbled.

She knew he went to work at one thirty in the morning and came home after two in the afternoon. He was the one who carried the big bundles of sugarcane to the flume. From there they floated downhill to the mill. Then he came home and worked on the piece of ground where he grew his own sugarcane to stretch the 90 cents-per-day wage.

She remembered the day he came home and told her mother, "Now we can grow cane to help pay store bill."

And her mother had smiled because all the things they bought came from the plantation store, and they never had enough money to pay. But their cane didn't grow fast. It was a year and a half before the foreman *(luna)* came from the company to weigh the cane and give them credit at the plantation office.

The sugar stalks suddenly rustled beside her, and she gasped as a big centipede crawled across the ground a few feet away. She got up quickly and pushed through the cane to a cleared area. Ugh, she hated centipedes. At home she and the others were always filling in the spaces between the wallboards with scraps of paper to keep out centipedes. A centipede sting could make a baby sick, maybe make it die, even.

A baby . . . she wondered what had happened to Mama's last baby, the one they gave away. She saw again the grief on her father's face.

"No can keep the new baby. No can look after him."

They gave him to a Korean couple with no children. For a while her father had made them all get washed and dressed on Sundays and walk three miles with him to visit their little brother. They played with him and sang to him. Then one Sunday they went and the family was gone.

"Gone to Korea," a neighbor said.

"Maybe they no like us visit," her father said.

Marita tried to picture the baby now. He must be six years old. How did he look?

"Mari-i-i-ta!"

It was her sister Blossom calling. The sun was going down; soon it would be dark. Already there were strange sounds around her in the dusk. She held the new shoes tightly against her chest and didn't call back. She would stay longer. Papa might go to sleep soon.

Her stomach made a hungry noise. She thought about her father's dinner. When he cooked, dinner was good. Maybe tonight they would have rice with pickled *daikon* or wild spinach and dandelion shoots. And after maybe a banana or two from the banana house. Bananas and mountain apples grew well in the gulch beside the camp.

Their neighbor, Mrs. Lee, said, "Grow good because toilet water run down the gulch."

Mrs. Lee was a good neighbor when she had time. She helped sometimes with the rice. Sometimes with the washing. Oh, that washing! How Marita hated to wash clothes!

What a mess that first time—she would never forget. . . . After Mama died there was only Marita to do the wash. Only Marita with her short arms and eight-year-old legs to carry the dirty clothes to the big bath on the outside fire and boil them. The way Mama did. She remembered to cut the brown soap small. But she forgot to put the clothes in two piles. She washed them all together, and what happened? The colors from Papa's dirty work clothes turned everything brown. She could still hear Papa shout, "See the mess! You never learn nothing from Mama?"

And again today he had shouted at her about the shoes. And often over the years he had shouted when she did things wrong. Only lately had she thought poor Papa must be lonely all these years. What a hard time he had. . . .

Even with the baby gone, Little Sister was still small—not even two when Mama died. She walked around the house touching everything. It was lucky for the family she was a happy baby and didn't mind having her leg tied to the table when the big kids went to school. They left rice in a bowl on the floor, pointed to it, and said, "Eat that for lunch."

There was no one to look after Little Sister then. She seemed content to stay by herself and never cried. But Marita wondered every day if Little Sister was all right. Now Little Sister was eight and running around like the rest. Pauly was eleven, Blossom ten, and Joe nine—they were all growing up. Pauly was the bold one. Sometimes she worried about him, too. He was the one who climbed the trees and crossed the streams and scooted down the gullies faster than his friends.

"Mari-i-i-ta!"

Blossom's voice sounded closer.

"Come home, Marita—Papa's in bed! Tomorrow he'll forget!" she called. "I saved you rice and vegetable."

Marita wrinkled her nose. She could almost smell dinner. She stood up and shook out her dress. It was faded blue gingham and short. Maybe she had grown again. She held the shoes to her chest and stepped out onto the path between two rows of cane.

"Okay," she called back.

Blossom waited at the edge of the field. Her dress was the same material as Marita's. Marita saw it, too, was short. Although Blossom was four years younger than Marita, her skinny brown legs seemed very long under that dress. Nice to have long legs. . . .

"Mrs. Lee came tonight," Blossom said. "With the stuff for new dresses."

"What color this time?"

"Red. With stripes."

Marita smiled. "Good. I'm tired of blue."

Once a year their father ordered a roll of cloth from the store. Mrs. Lee and Marita made it into whatever—dresses for the girls, shirts for the boys and Papa, curtains if they were needed.

"She said to come to her house tomorrow. Your dress is done."

They ran back to the camp. Marita ate the rice and vegetables, listening to her father and brothers breathing heavily in their beds. Then she and Blossom climbed into bed with Little Sister.

"No bath tonight," Blossom whispered. "Boys went to the bathhouse before they went to bed."

Marita thrust a dirty foot over the edge of the bed and felt a twinge of guilt. But just a twinge. Usually she enjoyed going to the bathhouse with her sisters, where the women and girls bathed on one side and the men and boys on the other. They would soap themselves first with the same brown soap used for washing clothes, then pour water over themselves to rinse, and then finally step into the big wooden box filled with hot water. But tonight before drifting off to sleep Marita was thinking about her graduation dress. It was the first truly pretty dress she had ever had. Mrs. Lee made it from a paper pattern. It made her look really nice. Papa paid for that, too. Well, one day she would buy things for him. When she got a job.

The next day after school Marita went to Mrs. Lee's.

"Door open," Mrs. Lee called when Marita knocked.

She went in and felt a tremor of excitement. There it was—the dress, hanging over a chair. Her dress, her graduation dress.

"Oh, Mrs. Lee, so pretty!" she exclaimed.

"Try," Mrs. Lee said.

Marita took off her old dress and slipped the new one over her head. Ah, the smell of it! So new, so fresh! She did up the buttons in Mrs. Lee's perfect buttonholes.

"How's it look?" she asked, and whirled around. The skirt swung this way and that in a satisfying manner.

"Nice," murmured Mrs. Lee, her head bent over another dress. "You like take today?"

Marita nodded.

"Keep clean," Mrs. Lee said, "for Friday."

Only two days to graduation. Marita took the dress home and hung it over the window-curtain rod. She put the new shoes on the floor beside it and went to make dinner. Tonight it was sweet potato leaves and rice.

Pauly and Joe ran across the compound shouting. Pauly was the pack leader, as usual. She saw them head for the big mango tree and shouted, "Bring mangoes for dinner!"

When the rice was on the fire she went back into the house to look at the dress again. She touched it, loving the soft new feel of it. Suddenly she had an urge to put it on. The new shoes, too. In a minute she had changed.

Dressed up like a queen, she thought, and tried walking on her toes to make herself taller. She saw her reflection faintly in the window and bowed.

Someone ran shouting to the door.

"Marita, come quick! Pauly cannot get down! In the big mango tree!"

Joe was wide-eyed and anxious. He grabbed Marita's hand and pulled her outside. They ran across the compound to a crowd of women and children around the mango tree.

"Look!" someone said, pointing up.

Pauly was way up there. Almost to the top. The branch he had climbed on must have been damaged in the last storm. Marita could see where it had cracked and now hung limply. Pauly was clinging to the branch just below the break.

"Marita, help me!" he called.

Without thinking she climbed up the tree as fast as she could. The shoes helped. In a few moments she reached the big branch where Pauly swung precariously. "No worry, Pauly," she said. "I got you."

He smiled for an instant.

"Be still; don't move," she said softly. She edged out on her stomach across the big tree limb. Her side of the branch was fine. The part Pauly was clinging to was not. It hung by what looked like just a few fibers of wood. She glanced down. It was a long way to the ground. The people below had become quiet.

She inched closer and closer to the broken end of the branch. The closer she got to Pauly, the more the broken branch creaked and swayed. "Hold on," she whispered. "It's okay."

Now she was near enough to reach him. Maybe.

She stretched out a hand toward Pauly. Not close enough. She moved forward again and felt the limb creak against her stomach. She could feel it bend down just a little farther. "Take my hand, quick!" she ordered.

His fingers touched hers.

"More!" She pulled herself another inch along the branch and this time clasped her brother's hand tightly. Lucky he's small, she thought, but he's still heavy.

Holding his sister's hand, Pauly shifted his other hand and grabbed the solid side of the branch. He pushed his feet against the broken section and eased his body up beside Marita. As he did so, the last few fibers broke, and the broken branch crashed down, scattering the people below.

"Okay now," Pauly said.

They climbed down the tree, helped by friendly hands the last few steps.

"No mango for dinner," Pauly said. "Let's go."

Marita gave him a sisterly push. "Stay out of mango trees," she said. "Lucky you no break your head."

"Marita, look at the dress!" Mrs. Lee exclaimed as they came back across the compound.

The dress! She'd forgotten the dress!

There was dirt all down the front and a tear in the skirt. And the new shoes were all scuffed. No longer new.

Marita felt the tears begin to prick behind her eyelids. What could she say to Papa?

Just then he came toward them.

"You okay?" he asked. She saw he was breathing hard, as if he had been running.

She nodded.

"Marita saved me!" Pauly shouted. "Climbed up after me. Without Marita I fall for sure."

Papa blinked his eyes two, three times. "Good girl, Marita," he said, and patted her shoulder.

"But the new dress, Papa," Marita whispered. "All ruined. And the shoes so expensive . . ."

Papa looked at her. Then he smiled. "You one good little mother, Marita," he said. "Mrs. Lee maybe can wash the dress and fix. The shoes I polish myself."

The Gulch Is Calling

When Pauly ran he thought he was flying. Surely this must be almost as good as being a bird. Running down the gulch was the closest thing to flying he could imagine. Running down the green, slippery path with his bare feet hardly touching the ground. Running and leaping over branches and roots all the way down to the bottom of the gulch and pulling himself to a breathless stop at the foot, just inches away from the stream. Then, after a quick splash, he would run up the path again to the top and stand there, panting and looking back down the trail he had come up. He had made that trail. Before him there had been nothing but bushes and shrubs and tall grass. He'd made it with his body and his long, thin legs that had plowed their way up and down so often, so that now there was a visible trail leading down from the back of the Korean field-workers' camp to the base of the gulch.

He ran every day after school and had a pact with himself that one day he would be the fastest runner in school. Faster even than some of the older boys. He might not be as big as they were—he was skinny and quite short for eleven, although his legs were longer than his body—but he knew he could be faster than any of them.

"Where you go after school?" his little brother Joe asked. "Never can find you."

"Busy," Pauly said.

He felt guilty about not telling Joe, but he didn't want him hanging around all the time.

Summer was almost here and the end-of-school race day with it. He checked the teacher's calendar in the classroom to see how much time was left to get his leg muscles hard and strong enough to win.

There was the hundred yard dash, the obstacle, and the relay. He knew he'd have to compete with a group of older boys, some of whom were good runners. Boys like Ross Cunningham and Jack Perry, whose reputations as athletes were well known in school. Jack Perry was the son of one of the foremen, and Ross Cunningham's family owned the plantation. Pauly had never spoken to Cunningham. He knew him by sight—tall and well built with blond hair and a cheerful face. Sometimes he thought he'd like to talk to him but then could never think of anything to say. Once he thought Cunningham was going to say something, but then, at the last minute, the boy turned away.

He'd heard his father talk about the Cunninghams. They were rich. Must be, to own the whole plantation and live in that big house. It was a white house with a porch all around the downstairs. It sat amid a wild garden fragrant with plumeria and ginger flowers on the bluff, above the camp. Pauly and his family lived in one of the camp shacks, and his father worked on the plantation cutting sugarcane. His father had come to Hawaii from Korea many years before and still spoke Korean most of the time.

"Boss' house like a king's palace," his father said.

Pauly thought the house was beautiful. He climbed up the other side of the gulch one day to see better and spied a woman in the garden cutting flowers. She was quite young and pretty, with red-gold hair and a pale blue dress. He stared at her through a hedge of hibiscus and heard Ross call out, "Hey, Mom!" as he ran across the garden toward her. When he reached her, his mother stretched out a hand and ruffled his hair. Watching them together, Pauly felt a lump rising in his throat. He could scarcely remember his own mother. Just a reflection of a face smiling at him years before. It seemed a very long time now since she had died. Some nights, when he lay in bed listening to Joe snoring softly beside him, he tried to remember what she looked like. But the picture was never clear. Only the warm feeling somewhere deep inside him was still real.

He was the oldest boy and was supposed to help his sister Marita with the chores. Sometimes he did, but often there was so much else to do. Things like playing marbles or agates with the other boys, or sliding down the gulch on ti leaves, or climbing trees, or looking for birds' nests—so many interesting things. And now there was his new project with the race . . . certainly not much time now to help Marita.

He heard her calling him one day as he came home from school, but the gulch was calling, too. He dropped his schoolbook by the back door and hurried off to practice. Marita's voice quickly faded into the distance.

It was a hot afternoon, and there was a hive of wild bees buzzing in one of the guava trees. Pauly heard their steady humming as he ran past the tree and could see some of them flying around a small hole in the trunk. Stupid bees, he thought. Why did they have to pick a tree right on *his* trail? Well—he'd ignore them and just keep running anyway. Up and down, up and down he ran, his bare brown legs working like two pistons. He was panting uphill for the sixteenth run when he heard some voices floating up from the gulch below and slowed down to listen.

"Come on, you guys, speed it up!"

The voice was Ross Cunningham's. He could see him now, loping along the edge of the stream, followed at a distance by Jack Perry and another of their group, Kenny Behr. They wore matching red cotton shirts, like a team. Pauly felt a twinge of envy. He would have liked a red shirt. All his shirts were made from flour sacks, and he had one nice one for Sundays when the family went to see his mother's grave.

The boys passed below him as he crouched behind a monkeypod sapling, scarcely daring to breathe. Then they were gone. He continued upward past the guava tree again, and it seemed to him that the bees were buzzing more loudly than before. They sounded different—almost as if they were angry. One dived at his face, and he swatted it away as he ran past. For a moment it seemed to be following him; then he outran it.

At the head of the trail again, he stopped briefly to peer down into the gulch, looking for a flash of red shirts moving below. But the only red was the vermilion of the African tulip tree's flowers. He plunged back down the trail again, building up speed as he ran. Exhilarated by his own energy, his feet were winged as he skimmed over the ground. Between bushes and trees, over the slippery grasses he hurtled, and there came the guava tree again. He had a glimpse of a noisy cloud of bees above him as he ran past and jerked his head back to see them better. He didn't see the dead branch until it was too late. He was falling and rolling, over and over, down the path with the bees diving at him. Another tree broke his plunge downhill, and he jumped up, beating at the bees with his arms and yelling "Ow!" as they stung him again and again on his face and neck, his hands, legs—it felt like everywhere. Still waving his arms wildly, he crashed down the path toward the stream, knowing he had to get to that cool water. Some of the bees were still following him, an angry, determined dark haze of them. Then he saw a flash of red up ahead and realized the three boys from school were down there.

"Bees!" he yelled. "Bees!"

He saw their faces looking up in surprise as he crashed down the trail toward them. The boys scattered just before he hit the base of the trail and jumped into the stream. How soothing and cool the water was. . . . His body was on fire with all the stings, but the water was like a lotion that slowly lessened the pain. He lay in the water for what seemed like a long time, covering his head and face as well and just coming up for air when he had to. He thought he could still hear the bees when he came up to breathe. Then finally all he could hear was the gurgle of the stream. He sat up and looked around. No sign of the other boys. He was glad they had gone. He must look a mess now. He could feel big lumps all over his face and neck. He pulled himself onto the bank and started to pluck out the stingers that were still in his arms and legs.

A sudden rustling in the bushes made him look up. Ross Cunningham walked over to him and stood staring.

"Wow," he said. And again, "Wow."

Pauly patted his face. He hurt like crazy all over but was determined not to show it. "Looks real bad?" he asked, his cheeks aching when he talked.

"*Real* bad," Cunningham said. "Better go on home and have your mother put something on those stings."

Pauly looked up at him. "Mother's dead," he said.

Cunningham looked down at the ground. "Oh, well—why not come home with me? My mom's got stuff that works great on stings."

He put out a hand to help Pauly up, but Pauly ignored it. He had half a mind to go home, but he knew they had nothing good for stings. His body still throbbed painfully.

"Okay," he said after a moment, then got to his feet.

The Cunningham garden still smelled of plumeria and ginger. Today Ross' mother was wearing a pink dress and a big, shady hat.

"You poor boy," she said as Ross explained about the bees. "Come into the house and let me put ammonia on those stings."

The inside of the house was even better than the outside. Quite different from Pauly's house. His was small and dark with a bare wood floor and no bathroom, and only a few old pieces of furniture. This house was cool and quiet with white walls and high ceilings and beautiful furniture. Pauly walked after Mrs. Cunningham, sneaking looks from right to left as she led him down the hall and across the spacious living room to stairs covered with rich, red carpet. Upstairs they went into a bathroom as big as the bedroom he shared with Joe. Everything was white tile and shiny metal—he had never seen anything so clean and perfect.

Mrs. Cunningham made him sit on a stool and then dabbed all his stings with something that made him sneeze. But the stuff helped, and the pain gradually dwindled.

"How about some lemonade and cookies, boys?"

They went back downstairs and into a large, airy kitchen where a ceiling fan moved lazily. Pauly had never had lemonade before but decided immediately that he liked it. The cookies had raisins in them and tasted good, too.

"You running in the races next week?" Ross asked between bites.

Pauly nodded.

"All three races?"

"Yeah."

"We've been watching you in the gulch. That's some training program you got. You learn that in Korea?"

Pauly shook his head. "Born here," he said. "Father came from Korea a long time ago."

"My father says the Koreans are real good workers," Ross went on. "Tough people."

Pauly grinned. "Yeah," he said. "You see me run?"

"Sure. Kenny and Jack and me run in the gulch every day. We knew you were running up and down that hill."

Pauly frowned. "Never saw you," he said.

"That's because we usually wear green and stay farther away," Ross said. "Today was the first day to wear our new red shirts. Like 'em?"

Pauly nodded.

"We've been looking for a number four for our team," Ross went on.

Pauly squinted up at him and then looked away again. Why

should Cunningham say that? It wasn't likely they would ask *him* to be on the team.

"Gotta go now," he said, getting up and brushing the crumbs off his face. "Thanks for the drink."

He gave a little nod to Mrs. Cunningham and ran out of the back door. All the way home he was thinking how much he would like to be on that relay team. Not just because of the shirt. What a winning team they could be! Well, he'd just go on practicing on his own and show them how good he was. Without them.

The last few days before the end of school went past quickly. Finally, the big day came. Another morning with the sun chasing the early morning mists out of the gulch.

Pauly was awake with the rooster's crow and lay in bed picturing the race field. There was the schoolhouse, and over there the main starting line; the finish way down at the end . . .

A sudden rustling on the porch outside broke in on his thoughts. What was that? He lay listening quietly—there it was again. Climbing carefully over a sleeping Joe, he tiptoed to the front door and opened it. There was a package wrapped in brown paper on the top step. Written on it in large letters was his name.

He snatched it up and ripped it open. Inside was a red shirt and a note—"Welcome to the team."

Grinning, he pulled on the shirt and ran down to the gulch for one last practice.

Guava Sticks

The afternoon was hot and still. Kona weather, people said. There was scarcely a breath of air moving in the classroom, although every window was wide open.

Blossom wriggled uncomfortably at her desk as she struggled with her schoolwork. She just couldn't get the characters to look right. And today, when her dress was stuck to her back with sweat and even her pencil felt slippery in her moist hand, she felt even less like concentrating. She looked out of the nearest window at the hot, blue sky and wondered what it would be like to paddle in the cool waters of the ocean.

She was enjoying the water frothing over her toes when she heard the teacher's voice. Mr. Chae had a raspy voice anyway, and now he said for everyone to hear, "Blossom Kim, pay attention to your work! You will stay after school again today."

Blossom sighed and bent her head over the paper again. How she hated Mr. Chae! Such an ugly, small man, too. Never smiled. How could you like anyone who never smiled? Every day he droned out instructions to the class and wrote what seemed like books of information up on the board for them to copy.

"Say after me," he would intone, and the class dutifully repeated whatever he said. Sometimes Blossom just moved her lips. It was never good to rebel visibly because Mr. Chae caned. He caned with guava sticks that he made the students bring to him.

"My sticks look tired," he would say. "Fetch some new ones tomorrow."

Blossom wondered how the sticks were today. Tired, she hoped. There was a good chance Mr. Chae would cane her legs after class, as he often did when the students were kept late for misdemeanors. She tucked her skirt tightly around her knees and tried not to think about it.

Mr. Chae was watching Blossom and saw her tuck her dress around her knees. He felt his lips twitch but managed to stop the smile from forming. Blossom was a fair student, and he knew she tried to do her work. Too bad she was a dreamer. It wasn't good to dream too much because dreams didn't come true. Hadn't he dreamed about the good life in Hawaii, a goal he'd had for years? Now here he was in a camp school teaching children from his homeland how to read and write Korean. What a hard task it was.

And hadn't he dreamed of a docile, willing wife who would cook and clean and bear children? And perhaps even be willing to share some of his interest in Korean studies? When he had courted his wife in Korea they had sat together on her father's clay floor, enjoying the warmth coming down the flue from the outside fireplace, and they had talked about Hawaii. He told her she would never feel truly cold again, and she had smiled. Where he lived there was sunshine and flowers all year round, he had said. She had seemed happy to marry him— what had happened?

When they got to Hawaii she changed. She gossiped and

spent his money and then left him because she said he was old and already half dead. She went off with a younger man to another island. People said she knew the man before, but Mr. Chae knew nothing about him at all. She had gone and that was enough. Gone and taken everything she had brought from Korea, plus all the items she had bought with *his* money. Everything was gone except a little silk fan he had found at the back of a drawer between two folds of paper. She must have missed it when she packed her things. He had kept the fan and liked to hold it occasionally. There was a faint scent to it that reminded him of his wife. He had absentmindedly put it in his pocket one day before he left for school, and now it lay wrapped in a scrap of cloth in the top drawer of his desk. He opened the drawer and felt for the fan. Yes, it was still there. He should really take it home.

Mr. Chae sighed and stretched his neck muscles. He was tired and supposed the children were also. They had already been in school with him early in the day, then had gone to public school in Hakalau, and now they were back with him again in the afternoon. Sometimes he thought it was all so much water down the gulch. Sometimes a student would surprise him by doing more than requested. Not often. And so far, Blossom had never fallen into that category. He decided not to use the guava sticks today, and felt better.

At the end of the class Mr. Chae said, "You can go now," and everyone left. Blossom sat still and waited. When was he going to cane her? Mr. Chae walked up to her desk and frowned. "You will memorize one more character before going home today," he said. "Saturday I will test you." He chalked a character on the board. "Copy that with the English meaning in your book three times and then you can go home. I will come back in a half hour." Then he walked out, and Blossom saw he had a large tear in the back of his loose cotton jacket. Shame! Didn't his wife sew for him?

She bent over her book and tried to concentrate on the character, but somewhere at the back of her mind a thought poked itself out. Mr. Chae's wife ... where had she heard something about her? Usually the adults didn't gossip much around the children. But one day Blossom had overheard two neighbors talking about Mr. Chae's wife.

"The schoolmaster got more than he bargained for when he married that young girl," one said.

The other sniggered and answered, "No wonder she left him—too old for her."

Maybe that was why the tear was in his jacket.

Laboriously Blossom copied the new character on the paper. It was a slow process. Mr. Chae demanded perfection, and she felt her work was far from perfect.

The minutes ticked slowly on the wall clock, but at last, with a sigh of relief, she finished and put down the pencil. Still more than five minutes before Mr. Chae would come back. ... Probably he'd cane her when he did come. Blossom had been caned before and could still remember the stinging whip of the guava sticks. Didn't want that again. ...

She pushed the fear aside and sauntered over to the teacher's desk. Nothing much on it. Two or three books and a tray with chalk and a few pencils. She ran her fingers along the desk front, feeling the rough texture of the wood. Her fingers touched a drawer pull, and before she could stop herself she had opened the drawer. Nothing much here, either. More papers, an eraser, a long ruler, and a small bundle wrapped in cotton cloth. She felt around the bundle but couldn't decide what was in it—without looking anyway. She unwrapped the cloth and saw a fan. It was very pretty, black silk stuff with lace on the edge. She opened it up and found a picture of a bird with a blue-and-green tail painted in shiny paint. She fanned her hot face, and a hint of fragrance came to her. Why did old Mr. Chae have a fan? Surely it couldn't be his. It was supposed to be a woman's. Or a girl's. Blossom ruffled the lace edging with her fingertip. Maybe he wouldn't miss it if she took it? Quickly she picked out two of the pencils that were about the same length as the folded fan and wrapped them inside the piece of cotton. The bundle looked the same. Then she closed the drawer and walked quickly away and back to her desk with the fan inside her dress clutched under one arm. Her heart was beating hard and she felt a trickle of sweat running down her temple. Footsteps. Mr. Chae was returning. Now for the caning . . . she clenched her teeth.

Mr. Chae walked briskly into the classroom and said, "I see you have finished. You may go now. I hope you have learned something."

Blossom eyed the guava sticks.

"No, I'm not going to cane you," Mr. Chae said gruffly. "Go on home."

Blossom stared at him in disbelief. Then she turned and ran before he could change his mind. She ran all the way home. Marita was outside buying a soup bone from the meat man's truck.

"Where were you?" she asked.

"School," Blossom answered briefly. "Teacher made me

stay." She hurried into the bedroom she shared with her two sisters and stuffed the fan under her side of the mattress.

Later that night, when they were all in bed, she lay thinking about the fan. She thought so hard about it that when she eventually fell asleep she dreamed about Mr. Chae.

"You're a thief, Blossom Kim," he was saying. He was standing over her waving a bunch of the biggest guava sticks she had ever seen.

She awoke shouting, "No! No!" and woke up Marita and Little Sister, who were in bed with her.

"Now you woke me up, you can come to the outhouse with me," Marita said. "Scared to go alone."

"Use china pot," Blossom said sleepily.

"No, gotta *go!*" Marita insisted.

They stumbled together through the living room, trying to be quiet and not wake their father, who lay snoring on the old sofa. They crept outside to the dark outhouse twenty feet behind the house.

When Marita was ready to go back to bed, Blossom said, "You go in. I like think a minute."

And Marita, who was half asleep anyway, just mumbled something and went back inside.

Blossom sat down on the porch step to think.

That dream scared her. What if Mr. Chae found out she took the fan? A scary dream was bad enough, but what if it came true? Maybe she'd better put back the fan right now. She tiptoed into the house past her snoring father and into her bedroom. Marita was already asleep. Blossom eased the fan out from under the mattress, stuffed it under her arm, and ran down the front steps. She headed for Mr. Chae's classroom in the camp.

Lucky it was a bright night. There was a full moon lighting up the countryside. After one look at the moon's face, with its two eyes and a nose showing clearly, Blossom decided not to look up there again. It was like someone was watching her. If she hadn't been so nervous and jumpy, she would have enjoyed the night, but there were strange shapes and shadows about and some unknown noises. The *lehua* trees looked like giant witches, and there were mysterious scrabblings coming from the bushes along the path. By the time she had almost reached the classroom Blossom thought that if anyone was around—don't let that happen!—they must surely hear her heart, which pounded in her ears like a noisy hammer.

Mr. Chae's little house was next door to the classroom; she gave the front door a wide berth. One of the windows was open, and there was a strange sound coming from it. Blossom stopped to listen. What was it? At first she thought it was like an animal—a dog, perhaps. It sounded like a dog that had been beaten and was exhausted from howling: a deep, low moaning sound broken by gasping or—sobbing? Blossom listened harder. Was that someone *crying*? She crept closer to the window, where she could hear more clearly. It was someone crying, but the kind she had never heard before. It was an adult—a man—crying. She knew it could only be Mr. Chae.

How strange, she thought. Why would a man cry? Poor man sounded so sad. Then she tiptoed over to the classroom door. As usual, it was not locked. The door creaked a little as she opened it, and she held her breath. No other sounds. She slipped into the room and over to the desk. The moonlight lit up the whole place like a lamp, and she found the cloth bundle immediately. Didn't even look like it had been touched.

She switched the pencils for the fan and rewrapped the bundle. In a minute she was back outside and running home.

As she climbed onto the bed, Marita half turned and asked drowsily, "Where you went?"

"See a friend," Blossom whispered.

"Yeah, yeah, yeah, sure," Marita said, and went back to sleep.

Joe and the White Dog

Joe was bored. He was sitting in the shade of the big mango tree polishing a kukui nut. He had been working on it for weeks off and on, and now it was nearly perfect. Kukui nuts took a very long time to polish, and this one had taken longer because it was very large.

He rubbed the nut alternately with sandpaper and a scrap of rag and every now and then added a drop of spit for luck. He stopped at last and examined the smooth, shiny surface with a critical eye. Not bad. His best yet. He would show it to Koa in school tomorrow. Koa was Hawaiian and knew a lot about kukui nuts.

"Make good leis," he had said. "My mother has one kukui-nut lei. Real nice."

Koa's mother, who sometimes came to school to help with the lunches, told Joe more.

"Kukui nuts from the candlenut tree," she said. "In olden days the Hawaiian people made oil from candlenuts. Kukui is special to Hawaiians."

She leaned down to show Joe the shiny black necklace she had around her neck. She was soft and kind and smelled of the plumeria flowers that she wore in her long, black hair. Joe liked her and wished she could be his mother. His own mother was dead, and he couldn't remember her at all—but he was sure she must have been warm and sweet smelling like Koa's mother.

Little Sister came toddling over to the mango tree. "Take for walk," she demanded, holding out her hand.

Joe sighed and stuffed the kukui nut with the sandpaper and rag into his pants pocket. He took Little Sister's warm, chubby hand in his own, and they walked down the road away from their house in the sugar field-workers' camp and on up toward the bluff.

"See bee! See bee!"

Little Sister pointed to a large, black carpenter bee that was buzzing around a fallen trunk. Joe guided her past the tree and quickened his step. He was not fond of bees. They walked on, past the African tulip trees and the huge monkeypod and along a narrow path leading up to the top of the hill. From the top Joe knew they would be able to see the long slopes of the volcano. He had never been up as far as the volcano, but he had heard stories about it.

When they were almost at the top of the path, he tugged Little Sister's hand and shouted, "Run! Fast to top!"

Her fat little legs ran as fast as she could make them go, and when they reached the top she collapsed in giggles on the grass. Joe stood panting for a moment, looking up at distant Mauna Loa. There was a misty cloud hanging over the summit so that all he could see were the volcano's sloping sides in the distance.

In school the teacher had talked of the fiery lava that the volcano spat out from time to time, but Joe couldn't even imagine what it looked like. The teacher showed them pieces of lava rock and said that once the black rock had been red and liquid. Joe couldn't picture that at all, and besides, it was frightening to think about. What he loved was the mountain itself, its slopes like a giant apron stretching down to the ocean. One day, when he was older, he would climb that mountain for himself and see what was at the top.

He walked along the edge of the bluff, kicking gently at the grass with his bare feet and thinking about climbing the volcano. He'd need real shoes; boots, maybe. And a pack so he could carry food and something to drink on his back. Maybe he'd better have a man's hat in case the sun was too hot up there. . . . He could see himself now, a big hat on his head and maybe a soldier's pack on his back, setting out to explore the unknown. His lips puckered in a whistle and he quickened his pace to a march. He forgot all about Little Sister.

She was humming a tune to herself and looking for bugs among the bushes. But it was a warm afternoon, and before long she began to get sleepy. She crawled under a shady bush and fell fast asleep.

Joe marched up and down the bluff whistling for a while, stamping on the ground with his imaginary boots and adjusting his imaginary hat. In his mind he was just climbing the last stretch before the volcano's summit when a tiny thought crept into his fantasy and dragged him back to reality. Little Sister! Where was she?

He ran up and down, calling for her as loudly as he could, in and out of the bushes and up and down the path. But there was no sign of her. He began to feel afraid. Where could she be? And how could he go home without her? Soon their father would be home from work and looking for them. They were the youngest and not supposed to wander far from home. He knew he should have watched her better.

"Little Sister, where you stay?" he shouted. "Come *now!*"

But she didn't come.

Then he saw a dog. It was a little white dog. It came bounding out of the bushes, tail wagging and a grin on its face. Joe knelt down beside it and put his arm around its neck. The dog licked his face. "Good dog," Joe said. "You seen my sister?"

The dog wagged its tail harder and licked his face again.

"You lost a sister, boy?" a woman's voice asked, so close by that Joe jumped. He turned around to see who had spoken.

The speaker was an old Hawaiian woman with white hair that contrasted with her brown skin. She was wearing a light-colored dress and had bare feet. Joe thought it strange for her to be there because he didn't know of any Hawaiians living around there, so close to the Korean camp houses. He had never seen the woman before.

He nodded. "She was here," he said. "Minute ago."

"What are you doing here, anyway?" the old woman asked.

"To see the volcano," Joe answered. "One day I like climb it."

The old woman smiled, and Joe liked the way her eyes lit up. "That's my mountain," she said. "It is very beautiful. Beautiful and powerful."

"You live around here?" Joe asked.

She nodded and waved a hand vaguely in the direction of the volcano. "Over there. Now—you want to find your sister? I think she's under that bush." She pointed down the path. Her white dog took off toward the bush, and Joe followed at a run.

The dog was sniffing among the undergrowth, its tail wagging furiously.

"No lick nose!" An indignant cry came from the bushes, and Little Sister staggered out, rubbing her face. The white dog bounded along beside her.

"Bad girl," Joe scolded. "You get lost and big trouble for me." He turned to the old Hawaiian woman, who was now sitting on a rock and fanning herself with a large leaf. "*Mahalo,*" he said to her, using the Hawaiian word of thanks that Koa used. He had an idea that he should give her something but couldn't think of anything to give. Then he remembered the polished kukui nut in his pocket. He fished it out. "Here," he said, handing it to the old woman. "For you."

She looked at him with a strange expression on her face. Then she took the nut and examined it. "Good job," she said. "You polished it well." She stowed it away somewhere in a hidden pocket in her shapeless dress. "Now I need a drink. Any water 'round here, boy?"

"Sure," Joe answered. "Wait and I go get some. Little Sister, stay here. Play with the dog. Back soon." He scampered down the path and back to the camp to find something to put water in to give to the woman. There was an old tin cup on the kitchen table. He snatched it up, filled it with water outside, and hurried back up the path. By the time he got back half of the water had spilled out in spite of the care he had taken.

The old woman was still fanning herself on the rock, and Little Sister was combing the dog with a piece of broken comb.

"Here's the water," Joe said, handing the woman the cup. "I spilled a little."

"*Mahalo*," she said. She sipped the water slowly, smacking her lips, all the while looking at Joe. "What do you know about the volcano, boy?" she asked.

"Just what teacher said in school," Joe replied. "Said it wakes up and spits out red hot stuff. But I never seen that. Maybe it's not true."

The woman laughed. "It's true," she said. "Very true. One day you will see for yourself. One day soon."

Joe didn't like the sound of that. "Soon? How soon?" he asked.

But the old woman just smiled and said, "You'll see. Before your next birthday. Now I have to go home." She eased herself off the rock and whistled for the dog.

"Thanks for finding Little Sister," Joe called after her as she walked off along the upper path.

She waved a hand without turning around. The little white dog followed her at a run, and the two of them disappeared among the bushes. Joe wondered again where she lived. He thought he'd ask Koa about her in school.

Next day during lunch he sat with Koa. When Koa's mother came over to talk with them, he asked her, "You know one old Hawaiian lady with long, white hair? She got a dog, too."

Koa's mother stopped patting her son's shoulder, her hand suddenly very still. "You saw someone like that, Joe?"

Joe thought her voice sounded different. "Yeah. Up the path outside camp yesterday. Little Sister and me went to look at the volcano." He didn't say anything about Little Sister getting lost because he was still ashamed. "She told me the volcano going spit red hot stuff soon again. Before my next birthday."

Christina Joy Pratt

Koa's mother's eyes opened wide. "What else?"

"Nothing much. I got her water. She was thirsty."

Koa and his mother were staring at each other, and Koa's mouth had dropped open. "The dog," he whispered, "was it a *white* dog?"

Joe nodded. "Little white dog. Real cute."

"My Lord," said Koa's mother, and sat down on the bench beside Joe. She slipped an arm around his shoulders and gave him a squeeze. He could feel her arm trembling.

"You know that Hawaiian lady?" he asked again.

Koa's mother nodded. "I know her," she said. "That was Madam Pele, the guardian of all our volcanoes. She always appears as an old Hawaiian woman with long, white hair. And always with a little dog. Good thing you fetched her water when she asked!"

Joe nodded slowly. The kukui nut had probably been a good idea too. . . . "I guess so," he said.

But all the time he was thinking the old woman came to warn him not to climb the volcano by himself. At least, not until *after* his next birthday.

The Little People

When Little Sister was six years old, she told her family, "Now I'm big my name is Puni. No more Little Sister."

So everyone in the family began to call her Puni except Joe.

"You always Little Sister to me," he told her, and because she loved Joe with an extra love, Puni just smiled.

For a long time Puni had wanted a doll of her very own. Hardly any of the girls in the camp had a doll, but Gertrude Lee had one, and Gertrude Lee took it everywhere.

"Why you take that doll everywhere?" the boys asked Gertrude Lee. A group of children were playing under the big mango tree.

"She's my child," Gertrude Lee said, hugging the doll to her. "Of course she stay with me."

It was an ugly doll with a stupid face, Puni thought. Needed washing, too. When *she* got a doll, it would be beautiful, too.

She thought a lot about the doll and what it would look like. Maybe long, gold hair and blue eyes like Iris Jensen or maybe black hair and brown eyes like her own. Whatever, it would be a very pretty doll with a pink dress. Pink was Puni's favorite color.

"I like one doll," she told Blossom, who looked surprised.

"Why? No need one doll."

"Just want one," Puni said, and closed up her lips tight. She wanted to tell Blossom that for once she needed to have something of her very own; something special that would belong just to her. For as long as she could remember she had shared everything with her two sisters. She wore their old clothes, shared the few school things, and she didn't even have her own bed. Gertrude Lee had her own doll *and* her own bed. When she mentioned this to Marita, she said, "Gertrude Lee an only child—no brothers or sisters. Of course she have her own bed."

"You never want one doll, Marita?" Puni asked.

"What for?" Marita asked. "Always have you and Joe and Pauly and Blossom. Four babies keep me busy."

Puni thought and thought about that doll—sometimes in school, when she should have been doing her lessons, and often in bed at night lying beside Marita and Blossom. The big question was how to get a doll. She had no money. Papa had no money to spare for dolls. He had made that clear.

"You need what? *Doll?*" he had said, and then frowned at her. "No money for dat kine thing. Money for food and clothes."

Joe gave her a little stick doll he had carved, with a kukui nut for a head. He seemed proud of his work.

"Thanks," Puni said, putting it in her pocket. How could she tell him this was not the same as a beautiful doll in a pink dress?

One day in the school yard she heard some Hawaiian children talking about a path down to the ocean. They said it had been made by the little people that didn't like to be seen.

"*Menehune* get mad if they catch you," one boy said.

"Why? What happens?" another asked.

"Bad things."

"They do good things, too," a girl said. "You know they build that place way down in the woods near the beach."

Puni wanted to know about that. "What kine place?" she asked.

"Just an old wall with plenty weeds. My mother said it's real *old*."

"Sometimes you can get them to give you presents," the first boy said, "if you leave them something."

"Presents? What kine?" Maybe there was a doll in this after all.

"I dunno. Things you want, maybe."

Puni could hardly stop from jumping up and down. "Where's the path?" she asked.

"Long way from the Korean camp," the boy said. "Too far for your legs."

Puni stood as tall as she could. "I can walk far," she said. "Tell me where."

"You know the path by the biggest canefield—goes down to the ocean? Past the graveyard."

Puni shivered. "Yeah," she whispered.

"Down there. Path goes two ways. *Menehune* trail goes to the beach."

Puni walked slowly away from the group and found a shady place to sit and think.

This could be her big chance to get the doll. But if it meant going alone, and past the graveyard. . . . She had been down that canefield path before with Joe, but never alone. With Joe it had been fine. He had just laughed and taken her hand when she was afraid to pass the graveyard.

"Dead people no do nothing," he said.

Maybe she should tell Joe about the *menehune* trail? She thought she'd ask him to go with her.

But when she asked him about it on the way home, Joe was in a hurry to play agates with the other boys. "Not today," he said. "'Nother day, maybe." Then he ran on ahead. "No go alone!" he called over his shoulder.

That did it. She was tired of people telling her what to do. Papa, Marita, Pauly, Blossom, and now even Joe, all telling her what to do. She would go by herself and see those little *menehune* people and ask them for a doll. So, instead of following the other children back to the camp, she lingered behind until they were out of sight and then set off for the big canefield.

The sun was hot, and she was glad when she came to the path that bordered the big field. She ran down the hill toward the ocean. It was a long path, with the water glinting way down below. She couldn't even see the beach yet because she was still too far away from the edge of the cliffs. But she knew the beach was there under the cliffs, so the gloomy path through the trees that she and Joe had once taken must be the trail made by the *menehune*. She didn't know much about these *menehune*, just that they were small and full of magic. And very, very old. Well, if they gave you things, they must surely be kind too . . . she hoped.

She ate some guavas off a tree heavy with fruit, taking care to eat some of the flesh with the seeds in case she got "stuck." The guavas were sweet/tart and delicious. Then she wiped her hands on her skirt and found the stick doll with the kukui-nut head that Joe had given her still in the pocket. She patted the doll and hurried on down the path.

Before she knew it she had reached the graveyard with its huddle of small stones. There were weeds growing around all the graves, and a tired paper lantern fluttered on a stick above one. It was very, very quiet. Puni held her breath and ran past quickly, her heart thumping so loudly that she thought it would come out of her ears. She plunged down the path and was soon among the trees above the cliffs.

It was gloomy and cool in there, with shafts of sunlight piercing the greenery. And quiet, except for the sound of her own feet crunching on leaves and twigs.

She came to a fork in the path and tried to remember which way she and Joe had gone down to the beach. What had the boy said?

"Path goes two ways. *Menehune* trail goes to the beach."

She looked at both paths but couldn't remember which one she and Joe had taken last time. Then she saw a small shell a few feet away. Maybe that path led to the beach.

A little way down the path she came to the wall the girl had spoken about. It was taller than she was, built of rocks and covered with green moss. There were wild purple orchids growing up one area and a clump of white ginger flowers. Puni picked a ginger blossom and stuck it in her hair. It smelled like sweet honey perfume. She walked slowly along the wall, feeling the furry moss with her fingertips. On top of the wall, on a flat stone, there was a beautiful papaya, fat and golden, sitting beside a rock wrapped in a ti leaf. Maybe this was the place you left gifts for the *menehune*?

Carefully she took Joe's stick doll out of her pocket and

stood on tiptoe to lay it beside the papaya. "Please get me one doll," she said out loud. "A beautiful doll in one pink dress. *Mahalo*." Then she crept behind a tree and sat down with her back against the trunk to wait for the *menehune*. She waited and waited until the sunlight through the trees grew fainter and fainter. Finally it was gone, and the woods became quite dark.

Puni was tired and hungry by this time. She stretched her arms up in the air and yawned, and her yawn sounded very loud in the stillness. Her eyelids were getting heavy, too, and her head nodded several times as she tried to stop from falling asleep.

Then she heard a sound. Footsteps. They were coming her way! Shaking, she curled herself up as small as she could behind the tree and lay waiting for the *menehune*.

They were coming closer . . . the branches by the path moved . . . a dark figure came around the tree . . .

"Joe!" Puni squealed. "You scare me!"

"Silly girl," Joe said. "I told you no go alone. Come on. Time to go home. We saved dinner for you."

Puni stood up and brushed off her skirt. "Wait," she said, and ran over to the wall. She picked up the stick doll and quickly hid it behind her back because she didn't want Joe to see. "We can go now," she said, taking Joe's hand. She felt much better now that he was there. Even passing the grave-yard was okay.

"If we run, we get home before Papa sees," Joe said. "No need tell him."

But Joe must have told someone, Puni thought later on. Because on her seventh birthday there was a little doll with a pink dress lying on her pillow when she woke up. Unless the *menehune* . . .

The Pineapple Cannery

Sometimes Marita thought she had been preparing food all her life. Well, almost all her life—since she was eight, when Mama died, and now here she was, fifteen and paring the eyes off pineapples in a canning factory in Honolulu.

Such a noisy place, with empty cans rattling down the chute every few moments. The tray boys jostled and shouted to each other as they pushed the hand trucks to and from the machines, unloading empty cans and picking up full ones. And the smell! The air was full of it. The sweet, cloying smell of ripe pineapple and fermenting fruit skins. A smell that stuck in her nose and clung to her whole body so that she could hardly wait to wash it off when her shift was over. Even with the big wraparound smock and cap that covered her head, the smell still seeped through to her clothes and her hair. As for her hands—would her fingers ever get used to the abuse they were taking?

Lucky for her the girls around her knew what to do and had shown her how to handle the fruit.

"Like this," a girl named Stella had said the first day. "See—put the left thumb in the *puka* and cut the skin with the knife in your other hand."

There was a long line of girls working at the moving belt bringing the pineapples from the paring and coring machine. The first ones in line had the job of trimming off any skin or eyes left by the machine, and then the others down the line sliced at the slicer and packed the fruit in the empty cans supplied by the tray boys. . . . Marita was a trimmer, and her left thumb already felt as if it would never be the same again. And she'd only been there a week! She groaned and wiggled the thumb cautiously. "Feels like it's broke," she grumbled to Stella.

"Gets better," Stella said. "Believe me."

Stella was a small girl, too, not much taller than Marita and slightly built. She was round faced and pretty and Japanese. Her white smock was so long it touched the tops of her shoes. She handled the fruit deftly and was much quicker than Marita.

"I never going to be good like you," Marita sighed. "You go real fast."

"You'll go fast too, soon," Stella said. "Already you go faster than last week."

Marita felt someone's eyes on her and saw Mrs. Chen, the forelady, frowning at her. Maybe she was too slow for the job! She grabbed another pineapple and zipped around it as fast as she could with the knife, then picked up another and did the same. There, she was getting better. Mrs. Chen was staring at someone else now.

"How you like Honolulu?" Stella asked.

"Okay. Different. Not like Hakalau."

Stella smiled. "Big, eh? Hakalau one small town?"

Marita nodded. "Just one street. One store and one school. And plenty cane trucks."

Stella nodded as if she knew. "Like Maui, too. My family's from near Wailuku. Where you living in Honolulu?"

Marita told her about the boarding house that was run by Pong Sook's sister down near the docks, and about the small room she shared with one of the daughters. "Sometimes I get homesick," she said. "This my first time away from home."

"Me too," Stella said. "I live with my auntie. She works second shift here."

There was a sudden loud crash somewhere behind them and everyone looked around. One of the tray boys had dropped a tray full of cans newly packed with pineapple slices and syrup, and the fruit was all over the floor. The boy quickly began to pick up the mess and dump everything into a nearby trash bin. Marita felt sorry for him when she saw Mrs. Chen strutting toward him like an indignant chicken.

"Big row," whispered Stella. "She's mad!"

The girls couldn't hear what was said, but Mrs. Chen's head snapped up and down and she glared fiercely at the boy while she berated him. He stood with head slightly bowed and said nothing. Marita thought he had a nice face. Once she thought she saw his mouth twitch in a smile, but then it was gone. When Mrs. Chen was through, he finished the cleanup by washing the floor with a wet mop, then pushed his cart back for more trays. As he passed Marita he caught her staring, and his right eye closed in a wink. She flushed and grabbed another pineapple.

At lunch break she and Stella went outside and found a shady spot under a shower tree. Stella had a little box with a *bento* lunch—two rice balls, pickled radish, and a small piece of fish. Marita had rice and kimchi and a slab of Portuguese bread.

"You like share?" Stella asked.

"Okay. You like some bread?"

"How come you get Portuguese bread?" Stella asked. "You're Korean, right?"

"Sure," Marita answered. "But we got the Bread Lady back at the camp. She married one Korean man and now everybody like Portuguese bread. Good stuff!"

She thought about the family back home. It seemed a long time since Pong Sook had said, "Why not go to Honolulu, work in the cannery? Girls make good money there. You can stay with my sister's family—I can arrange it. Then you can send money home to help your father."

Surprisingly her father had agreed, saying the other kids were old enough to manage without her. Even Puni was growing up and had become quite independent. And Blossom knew how to cook rice.

They had all stood in a row by the house steps when she was ready to leave. The camp foreman was taking her in his car down to Hilo to catch the boat to Oahu, and she was very nervous. So nervous and excited she could scarcely hold her little parcel of belongings. Her father patted her shoulder and said gruffly, "No give Pong Sook sister trouble now."

And her own words—"No trouble from me. I send money every week."

Last week she'd sent the first money, feeling proud at the post office when she bought the money order. She had tried to imagine the look on her father's face when the money arrived.

Sitting there under the shower tree Marita could almost feel she was back home and this was school lunch—if it hadn't been for the cannery buildings and the heat rising off the tarmac in the parking lot. Then the trade winds sent a shower of peach-colored petals down on both girls. Marita took off her cap and shook her thick hair free to cool off.

"Hot," she said.

"I saving for one new dress," Stella said. "Red. New style."

"How much?"

"Six ninety-five. I got three fifty saved already."

"Lucky! I send most of my money back home. I only keep little bit. Enough for room and food."

"You got nothing to spend?"

"Yeah, maybe two dollars pay day."

"You like go shopping after work Saturday?"

When Saturday came, Marita could hardly wait for the morning to be over. They worked until one thirty and then were free. She and Stella gobbled down their lunches and hurried back to the pineapples whenever the whistle blew.

"Not long now," Stella whispered after Mrs. Chen walked past. "You think Mrs. Chen shops too?"

They both looked at Mrs. Chen's ramrod-straight back and sensible shoes and shook their heads.

"Too stiff to try on dresses," Marita said, and they both giggled.

After work they scrubbed their hands and splashed their faces; Stella combed her short, silky hair so that the flat look caused by her cap disappeared. Marita's hair was thicker and coarser, and she had tried to curl the front with two rag strips the night before. She thought it looked okay. "Some day I going get one perm," she told Stella. "Curly hair so nice."

She checked her wallet in her dress pocket one more time. There was the five-dollar bill to go to her father Monday, two whole dollars for herself to spend, and the rest for Pong Sook's sister. She felt rich. Never mind the smelly pineapples—she had money! One day she would go back to Hakalau in a big car filled with gifts for everyone. She would have permed hair and high-heeled shoes and maybe even painted nails. . . .

"Come," said Stella. "Chinatown not far. Only a few minutes' walk." She walked daintily, taking her steps with care and skirting around any piece of litter on the sidewalk. "What made you come to Honolulu?"

"Pong Sook said to go." Then Marita told her about the family, about Pauly and Joe, about Blossom and Puni and her father. Stella listened.

"You no more mother?" she said at last.

So Marita told her about Mama dying and how they had to give away the last baby.

Stella's eyes filled with tears. "Oh," she said. "So sad."

They were walking along the river now, and Marita thought how different it was from the streams back home. There the water was clear and lively; this was a dark, slow-moving stream that flowed down from the mountains behind the city, down between the tin-roofed houses and shops and slowly out to the great ocean. Even the ocean here looked different, as if it had been tamed and taught how to behave better.

As they approached Chinatown the streets became busier and noisier. There were automobiles and trolley cars and people everywhere. Stores opened on to the street with wares stacked high along the sidewalks. There were paper boys and shoe-shine boys on every corner. Stella pointed to the entrance to an open market. "We go there," she said, tugging Marita's skirt. "All kine stuff."

The market was a collection of dozens of different stalls selling fruits, vegetables, flowers, meat, fish (FRESH—STILL CAN SWIM), and wonderful, strange foods that Marita had never seen before.

There were live chickens in cages for discriminating shoppers who didn't want to buy a dead one, and there were ninety-five varieties of meats and fish displayed on beds of ice. The beady eyes of a decapitated pig looked at Marita from one showcase, the lackluster stare of a large fish from another. Everywhere there were people discussing prices, stuffing shopping bags, counting out money, advertising their wares ("Roast pork special today!"). And the wonderful smells of all kinds of foods . . . Marita wrinkled her nose in appreciation.

"Smell good," she told Stella.

They were passing a stall covered with raw meat. Stella made a face. "Some things better than others," she said.

"Look!" Marita said. "Tripe! We used to buy from a truck Fridays. I had one hard time cleaning it!"

"You like tripe?" Stella sounded amazed.

"Sure, when you cook it right. I learn to cook some from my father—tongue, liver, kidney, cheek meat, ox tail—even pig feet."

Stella shuddered. "I like eat but no can cook," she said, giving Marita an admiring glance.

They passed sacks of rice and flour, bags of dried fish (weird smell, Marita thought), tea in colored boxes, jars of pickles and seeds, rice cakes, and some small cookies that Stella explained were fortune cookies.

"You mean, people believe the paper in cookies?" Marita asked incredulously.

"Sure they do."

How could a cookie know your fortune? Marita shook her head.

They went up to a *manapua* stall and bought two of them—white, doughy, and filled with red pork. They tasted delicious. Then they bought one paper cup with lemonade and took turns drinking until the last sweet/tart drop was gone.

"Now what?" Marita asked.

Stella wiped her fingers carefully on her skirt. "The dress. You gotta see the red dress. This way!"

They ran back out to the street, and Stella made for a small dress shop that had six or seven dresses on stands crowded together in a display window. One of the dresses was red.

"That one," Stella hissed, pointing quickly. "Beautiful, yeah?"

It certainly was. Marita thought it was the most beautiful dress in Honolulu. It was made of soft, silky stuff and had a full skirt and a cute little white lace collar. "Oh, Stella," she sighed. "It's just wonderful."

"Red look good on you," Stella said. "Maybe you can get one too?"

Marita shook her head. How could she get the money? She pulled out her wallet and slowly counted out what she had. This for her father, this for Pong Sook's sister, this for her to spend. Only two dollars. Maybe she could buy it some time soon . . . wait a little longer and save some more . . . but the dress was *so* pretty. . . .

She put the wallet back in her pocket and looked up in time to catch the eye of a boy leaning against the doorway of the

restaurant next door. He had a broom in one hand but didn't seem to be doing any sweeping. He looked familiar.

Stella nudged her. "He's the tray boy who dropped the tray last week," she whispered. "Remember?"

Marita remembered how he had winked at her and blushed again. What was he staring at, anyway? She lifted her nose in the air and turned to Stella. "We go look at your dress," she said.

Just then she felt a tug on her skirt, and two people ran past her and on down the street. The second person was the tray boy. Quickly she felt in her pocket, but the wallet was gone.

"Hey!" she yelled. "You stole my money!"

She took off after the tray boy as fast as she could, leaving Stella to follow if she wanted to. She chased him for two blocks and then lost him on the main street where the crowds were too dense and she was too short to see ahead. She stopped and leaned against a doorway, panting and crying with frustration and anger. How could such a terrible thing have happened? All of her money gone and none to send home or give to Pong Sook's sister! She felt sick to her stomach.

"There you are!" Stella grabbed her arm. "I thought I lost you! What happened?"

"He took my money—that tray boy! We gotta find him and get it back."

They walked back the way they had come and eventually reached the restaurant next to the dress shop. The same boy was in the doorway!

Marita launched herself at him and began punching wildly at his chest, which was as high as she could reach.

"No need for that," the boy said, and grasped her wrists to stop the blows.

"What you mean no need?" yelled Marita. "You take my money, you—you thief!"

"No, I did not take your money! I got it back for you. Stop hitting me and I'll give it to you."

Marita stopped in disbelief. He handed her the wallet.

"Count it and see if it's all there," he said. "I chased the thief four blocks before I caught him. I saw it all from the time you took out your money and counted it until the boy took it. You were dumb to show off your money."

Marita and Stella counted the money. It was all there. Marita looked at the boy suspiciously. "How I know you telling truth?" she asked. "Maybe you take the money."

"I don't do this for fun," he answered, pointing to a lump on his chin that was already turning blue. "This is where he hit me."

She looked at his shirt. It was dirty—maybe after rolling in the street? She didn't know what to say. This was the most embarrassing thing that had ever happened to her. She looked at Stella, who raised her eyebrows and nodded.

"You could say 'thank you'," the boy said, grinning.

She managed a smile. "Thank you. I thought my money gone forever."

"Okay," he said. "Take more care next time. See you girls Monday."

He winked at both of them and went into the restaurant.

Stella nudged Marita. "Honolulu not so bad after all, maybe? I think you found another friend."

Abuji

The old man knew he was dying. They had brought him to the hospital the day before—or perhaps the day before that. He couldn't remember. The pictures and feelings kept him too occupied to care. He was living through the old days again and worried about the wall that somehow wasn't finished. The wall that had taken so long to build, so many hours in the hot Kaimuki sunshine.

Away in the distance someone said, "Drink a sip of this, Abuji."

But he wanted to think about Kaimuki. . . . He could feel the sun on his back again, and a great strength returned to his arms and shoulders. Thud, thud—he was swinging the mallet against the rock and felt the shaft shudder suddenly, throwing some chips of stone across the yard.

The Portuguese man who was building the wall worked under the shade of the big mango tree, but he, too, was sweating. Abuji could see the sweat running in trickles down his bare back. He wiped his own sweaty brow and rested the mallet against a large rock.

It must be nearly time to eat. He'd been out in the yard since early morning. He stretched his arms and pushed his shoulders back.

"Quite tall, old Abuji," he'd heard neighbors say. "Strong for his age. Cracks rock like a young man."

"Worked all his life," his daughter said. "Sure to have a strong back."

Abuji lived in a little house behind his daughter's house. He didn't want to be with the family all the time. Often he liked to sit in the yard beside his vegetable garden and look at the plants.

"What you doing, Harabuji?" his grandson asked.

"Hear the lettuce grow," Abuji answered.

The boy put his ear to the ground.

"No hear nothing," he said. "You joking."

His grandsons were real Americans, both born in Honolulu. They couldn't even speak Korean. It was lucky he spoke a little English.

He remembered when he first came to the Islands and how little English he knew. Just the few words he had learned on the boat from Korea in the Bible woman's classes. The boat trip was a lifetime away. Almost forty-five years since he had left Korea. He thought about going back. He thought about it often. And working there in the yard with the Portuguese man gave him an opportunity to think. He had been saving his money for a long time to go back to Korea. Not for a visit; for a mission.

"I'll give you some money, Abuji," his daughter said. "My own money."

"No need yet," he told her. "Next year, maybe."

But he knew then that the time was coming, because there was almost enough money and the wall was almost complete.

The Portuguese man stopped working and stood back to survey his wall. "An okay job, eh?" he asked with pride.

Abuji nodded. "Good okay job," he said.

They had been working together on the wall for a year, off and on. The Portuguese man had another job as well, and Abuji had three small gardening jobs in Kahala.

It had been a big project, that wall, to make it three feet high all around the big lot, and to make it by clearing the rocks from the lot itself. Big rocks that had to be split. Both men did the splitting, but Abuji did most because he lived there. The Portuguese man was adept at fitting the stones together and fixing them in place with cement.

"How's your blisters?" the Portuguese man asked.

Abuji held out his leathery hands. "Tough hands," he said. "No more blisters."

Not like when he first came to Hawaii and went to work in the canefields. Then he had blisters upon blisters and hands so sore he had wrapped them in rags. Working in the canefields was new to him then, a city boy from Korea. He had seen the poster promising jobs in Hawaii at almost one dollar a day. In Korea in 1905 that sounded good.

He remembered the overcrowded boat from Korea, with food scarce and monotonous and the smell of vomit lingering everywhere. When they reached Hawaii he was herded with the others through the immigration process and then picked up with another twenty men by a *luna* for a Big Island plantation. He could see himself and the others now, standing in line, scarcely daring to breathe as the *luna* looked them over.

His daughter's voice came shrilly from the house. "You like eat now?"

The Portuguese man was already sitting on the ground, his

back against the mango tree, eating something from a brown paper bag.

Abuji put down the mallet and walked over to wash his hands under a faucet outside the kitchen window.

"Rice and kimchi now," his daughter said through the window. "Chicken tonight."

Rice and kimchi were still his favorites, and she made good kimchi. He couldn't remember when she learned to make it, but he did remember the years he cooked. The years after his wife died having the last baby. Leaving him with six children, Marita the oldest at eight. Now she was—how old? Must be thirty-five. Still pretty and still rushing about the way she always did. She had three children of her own now, nice kids who never bothered him much. He enjoyed watching them and listening to their talk. He bought them candy. Now he had time for children, not like with his own. Those years after his wife died ran together now, filled with work and more work. No time to talk with the children when he came home. Except to scold for chores not done. . . .

Now he was climbing the short flight of steps outside the kitchen door at Kaimuki. . . . He looked over his shoulder. The Portuguese man was wiping his mouth on a big handkerchief, which he then put over his face, and leaned back against the tree. He did the same thing every day he worked.

"Time for my nap," he always said. "Help me feel good."

After he ate, Abuji walked across the yard to his shack for his pipe. He filled it carefully and sat in the doorway, puffing gently, feeling relaxed. Still seemed like a luxury sitting at his own doorway. Just smoke, without worrying or even thinking. But he couldn't stop thinking, could he? Times like this

he liked to think of the early years when he and Chur got married and of how happy he had been. After all his lonely years in Korea and then in Hawaii, he finally had a wife and a home. She had a sweet face. . . . He remembered the first picture he saw, before she came from Korea to marry him. An oval face with the trace of a smile, eyes modestly cast down, smooth hair. She had been twenty-one years old, many years younger than he. He carried the picture with him when he went to meet the boat so that he would know her. She might not recognize him from the picture he had sent because it was an old photograph. But she had recognized him. They stood there looking at each other on the dock, without speaking, and he thought what a pretty wife she would make and how proud he would be of her. They would have many children together. She already had a little girl of her own, a tiny thing clinging to her mother's skirt who looked at him with wide, frightened eyes.

His new wife fixed up the three-room plantation house they were given. Before she came he had lived in a bunkhouse with the other single men. After they had a small house for themselves. With her little daughter they were already a family. Chur sewed curtains from rice sacks and kept the place neat even after the babies came. She swept the bare wood floor every day and had a way with cooking that made rice and spicy vegetables extra good. She never talked about her life in Korea, only of her desire to leave for a new life in Hawaii. There had been a husband somewhere in the past, but all she said was, "Husband was no good for me and the child—no treat us right. His family sent us away."

Abuji drew on his pipe, savoring the memories. For several years they were happy. Then Chur died. She was young and seemed strong, but it was the last baby that killed her—another boy, and big. The neighbor had come running out to the canefield to tell him of the birth.

"Didn't want help," the woman said. "Baby came okay. Cut the cord herself."

But three weeks later she was dead. Dead and left him alone. The grief swept over his body again as he remembered first the agony and then the anger. The anger that only got better when he worked, hacking at the cane until his arms felt like bands of steel.

The baby lived, and he was in despair as to what to do. He couldn't stay home and care for it, and Marita was only eight; Little Sister not even two yet. They tried together for a week, but it was impossible.

"The boy will die," the Parks said. They were an older couple with no children. "Give him to us and we will look after him."

How was he to know that within a few months they would go back to Korea and take his son with them? The anguish of the day he heard the news, and the anger again. . . .

He tapped his pipe out on the step and stomped on the ashes. Often he wondered how he had endured the years after Chur's death. Years when he felt nothing but a numbness inside that even his children hardly penetrated. But always there was work.

Over the years he thought often about the boy, his son in Korea, and in his heart he knew he would one day go to look for him. One day.

The money he was saving grew very slowly. Every time he

went to the bank to add his gardening money, the clerk smiled at him.

"You're a good saver, Mr. Kim," she would say, and he would nod.

At last there was enough, and when he told Marita she said, "I'll give you more. Then you'll have more than enough."

It was a good time to go because the wall was almost done, all but the last few feet, and the Portuguese man said not to worry. He would finish it himself. "No *pilikia*," he said.

Just then Abuji felt someone trying to lift his head, and he relaxed against the hand. A wave of dizziness came and went. Just like being on the ship, he thought. His memory spiraled back to his second boat trip, this one to Korea to look for the boy. This trip by boat was very different from the one so long before. This time he had his own bunk in a cabin with just three others, and the meals were well cooked and plentiful. But the journey was still long, and he found the period of inactivity tedious. He walked around the deck over and over again and heard the crew say, "Look at that old boy—sure is fit!"

And he was, for a man of seventy-four. Still strong and never been sick a day in his life. He told Marita that a mixture of hard work and kimchi were the best medicine, and she seemed to feel the same way. Hardly looked more than twenty-five, although her eldest was already fourteen.

The ship docked in Japan, and he took another to Korea. Most of the time on board he thought about how he would begin looking for the boy. All he had was an old address from a neighbor at the camp and the new name Mr. Park had given his son, Yong Chun.

When he reached Pusan he was discouraged immediately.

The place was much bigger than he remembered and swarming with people. He found the address on the paper, but there was no house.

"Pulled down a long time ago," someone said.

Long time ago . . . long time ago . . . long time ago when you gave away the boy. . . . He could feel the damp shirt sticking to his back again as he walked down the crowded streets asking people around him, "Do you know Yong Chun Park? Came from Hawaii twenty-seven years ago?" Over and over again the same questions, but only head shakes and strange looks in reply. For the first time he was afraid he might not find the boy. After all these years of hoping and believing. That was when he thought about the wall again—how he and the Portuguese man had worked so hard to put it together, each piece fitting into a simple yet enormous pattern. He had been patient working on the wall, knowing that one day it would be complete. He would try to be patient now.

For three weeks he searched and talked and asked and hoped and met with many people who had been in Hawaii in the past. Then one day someone said, "I think I know the man." Someone who was a friend of a friend who had met a man in church who had spent years in Hawaii when he was younger. Now he was old and the wife dead. But the boy, he said, was a fine man.

Abuji could feel again the rough cloth of the man's coat as he had grasped it. "When can I see him?"

He could see the boy again standing in front of him now, not smiling but shy. Tall and well built and with the same long face as his own. He could feel the tears running down his cheeks and a deep sob rising in his chest. The boy reached out, pulling him against him, and they stood with their arms about each other for a long time, both of them crying for all the lost years.

"Time for your pill, Mr. Kim," a voice said, closer this time. Someone in white was leaning over him. Of course, he was in the hospital. . . . He looked past the nurse and saw Yong Chun's face beyond.

There wasn't much time left, Abuji knew, and he had things to do. Yong Chun's face leaned down toward him, and he tried to reach up to him. Surely the boy would understand if he had to go away for a while. He couldn't stay because the wall was waiting for him back in Kaimuki. The Portuguese man somehow hadn't finished it after all—he could still see a small gap. He knew he would have to finish it himself.

So there he was, back in the yard at Kaimuki with the hot sun on his back again and the mallet swinging in his hands. It was the last rock. Slowly and steadily he swung the mallet and felt the shaft shudder sweetly as the rock split, sending some chips of stone flying. He put down the mallet and flexed his shoulders. Then he picked up the last rock and placed it in the gap. It was a perfect fit.

ABOUT THE AUTHOR

Eve Begley Kiehm came to the United States from her native Scotland as a young woman. A freelance writer, she has a master's degree in history and French from Glasgow University. She is the author of several children's books and a nonfiction book for adults. Her interest in immigrant life in Hawaii dates from her introduction to the culture of her husband, Dennis, a Korean American. The couple, former residents of Hawaii, now make their home near Portland, Oregon.

ABOUT THE ILLUSTRATOR

Christine Joy Pratt, a Hawaii resident, is a graphic designer and illustrator.